Run

Craig Ditchfield

For Bazza

ACKNOWLEDGMENTS

Thank you to my mum for helping me edit, my dad
for helping me with the illustration, and
Miss Christina and Mrs Miner for helping and giving
me a chance to do nanowrimo.

1. SCHOOL ENDS

I saw the clock ticking. Ten seconds. Ten seconds until school was done. My heart was pounding. I looked at Jack.

"Five seconds," he whispered.

I heard the count down. "Three, two, one, zero."

The dreaded school bell rang. It sounded like a werewolf scraping his fingers down a blackboard.

We all picked up our stuff and ran for the door.

I had been dreading this moment since fifth grade. Jack and I ran for the school gates. Jack asked, "How long till you leave to America?"

"Tomorrow," I said with my head hung low.

"Come on man, you're my only friend," he said

"Jack, the new kids will be cool. Just act normal and I'll talk to you on WhatsApp every day."

"See you tomorrow Scott," he said.

"See you Jack," I said.

I walked up the stairs to my house.

When I got in I ran to my room. There was already a WhatsApp message from Jack.

I walked to the kitchen where my mum was.

"Hey mum."

"Hi Scott."

"What's for dinner?" I asked curiously.

"Pizza takeaway. I just sent the kitchen stuff to the USA."

"Can I go to Jack's house?"

"Yeah, okay, see you. Be back at seven for dinner."

I ran to Jack's house. He was on the steps of his house.

We left to the town centre.

I had brought ten pounds.

"Want to go to the hot dog stand?" I asked.

"Yeah," he replied.

We got two hot dogs. We sat on the bench. We sat there eating our hot dogs in silence. "Why do you have to leave?"

"I've said this ten times. It's my dad's job. It's not only you who doesn't want me to move."

"Do you want to go to the park?"

"Yes I do."

When we got there we played tag. There were other kids.

After a while we left.

When I got home my mum and I sat down to have dinner.

I didn't really want to eat anything. But I ate my pizza because it just sat there and made my smelling senses tingle.

We were watching a crummy TV show. It was about people singing in front of judges. I think it was called "The X Factor".

2. THE MOVE

It was Friday and I was walking down the stairs for the last time ever to have breakfast in this house.

After I had breakfast I asked mum, "Hey mum what time do we leave?"

"We leave at 3:00 pm."

"Can I go round to Jack's house?"

"Yes, but make sure you're back in time."

"Cool, see you later."

When I arrived at Jack's house I told him how much time I had. We played on his Xbox and PS3.

Eventually I had to leave.

When I got home it was already 2:30.

We had to pack the last things into our bags and say goodbyes. I saw Jack arrive. I ran to him and said my goodbyes and hopped into the car.

Mum and I drove away. That was when the salty taste hit my tongue.

We were going to London Heathrow airport.

We lived about three hours away. It was a long drive. To pass time I decided to play on my iPhone.

When we arrived we gave our car to the people that wanted to buy it and we left for the plane.

We found our plane that went to Detroit. We had a quick phone call to my dad and sister. My sister had to go in the middle of the phone call to go to the bus stop to ride to her college.

Mum and I got on the plane. There were TVs on the plane. I watched my favourite movie, "Mud".

Then I decided to catch some down time. When I woke up we were ten minutes to arrival.

My school started in seven weeks.

I wondered what I would do in that time having no friends.

My mum was awake and asked "Aren't you hungry? You didn't have dinner." I wasn't really hungry.

I wondered if there was a running team there.

One thing I was really happy about was the fact that there was a river five minutes away. I loved to swim. It made me happy and refreshed.

We were just landing.

When we landed people started to applaud.

We finally stood up to get off the plane.

Everyone stood up and this one crazy man started pushing his way through the crowd. He pushed my mum over. I was really angry with him now.

I went up to him and got in his way.

He was screaming at me to get out of the way.

He was screaming, "There are so many people".

"Hey, why did you push my mum?" I growled.

"Is it your business kid?"

I pushed him back and yelled: "I don't care if you're claustrophobic you don't push my mum."

"You don't tell me what to do and not do!"

Then my mum came and said "It's not worth getting in a fight with idiots like him."

"I'm not an idiot," he roared.

Now he was really pumped up.

Two men came and told him to calm down and he left me and my mum alone.

My mum and I had an awkward time from then on.

We went to get our bags and left for the front of the airport. My mum was on the phone to dad.

My dad was there. I ran at full pace. I jumped up at him. He caught me in the middle of the air.

"Hey sport," he exclaimed. "Mum sent me a text about what you did!! Good job."

We all got in the car.

"How long is the ride home?"

"30 minutes," he grumbled.

3. MEETING THE TOWN

When arrived we all helped unpack.

My dad told me there was a new kid who was also thirteen living across the road.

We all got in and I saw my bedroom. It was small but it was alright.

I put up my belongings up and started to make my bookshelf and bed. My sister's room was already made up because she had come here a month earlier.

I went downstairs.

I asked my mum and dad if there was a running team. They didn't know because they had never checked.

I decided to go upstairs and set some more stuff up. When I arrived at my room I look out of the window.

There was the new kid.

I ran down the stairs and went outside and ran to him.

"Wow, you're fast," he spluttered.

"Thanks. I bet you're fast too," I said.

"Do you want to go check out the town?"

"Yeah."

We walked around until we saw these guys pointing at us.

Then a guy who looked 16 walked over.

He had a big scar on his face.

He walked up to us. "I see we have two more little losers in town," he growled.

"Who you talking to?" I said sternly.

"You two losers."

"If there's a loser here it's you."

"Guys get them."

"Run!" I screamed.

We both ran full speed down the road.

The guy with the scar chased us and his gang followed him.

While we were running, I asked "What's your name?"

"Quinn."

"Cool, I'm Scott."

"Who's that behind us?"

"Scar."

We kept running.

"There's a busy road in front, we can lose them by running through and hopefully they'll get stuck behind some cars," said Quinn.

We ran and quickly crossed the road.

Luckily there were cars that came and stopped Scar and his gang from getting to us.

We started walking home.

"How long have you been here?" I asked Quinn.

"One month," he replied.

"So you've met him before?"

"Yeah, he's the big bad guy around. He hates me because he was bullying a kid and I threw an apple at him and it hit bang on his nose and his nose burst into a red volcano."

"Where did he get his scar from?" I asked.

"He got in a fight with this other gang in another town. Apparently a man had a knuckleduster and knocked him cold with one punch."

We decided to walk home.

Eventually we arrived.

"I'll see you around Quinn."

"Yeah."

When I got home I told my parents about what happened and they told me to be careful.

I went upstairs to get a look outside.

I looked out of my window and saw Scar and his gang.

They were walking to Quinn's house. I saw him at his window.

He looked up at me and I shook my head in the "no" gesture to tell him not to open the door.

I got my BB gun and loaded it.

Quinn had his at the ready as well.

He held up three fingers and pulled them down, on one he mouthed "go".

We both did rapid fire.

I saw one guy start screaming and then another.

We were hitting them.

Scar pulled out a mini BB gun and fired at me.

His gang also pulled out BB guns.

I saw Quinn duck. I did too.

I looked back and saw he had got a scope on his gun and I did too.

We were unstoppable.

Then I heard the siren song.

The police were coming. I put my BB gun back.

I saw them all run for it. I decided I would call that a day.

4. EXPLORER

I woke up.

Six weeks until school exactly.

I called Quinn. I asked him if he wanted to go to town.

I got my breakfast and went upstairs, got my phone and stuck my hand BB gun in my bag.

I also got 20 dollars, a torch and a rope.

We left the house and walked to town.

"Hey Quinn, when's your birthday?"

"September 10th."

"Three days."

"Cool."

"What will you do for the birthday party?"

"Dunno."

"What are you getting?"

"A motocross."

We kept walking into town and stopped by my mum's Ben and Jerry's shop and got an ice cream.

Then he told me about this epic hideout he has.

We walked to this dump yard and went to this train.

"This is it," Quinn said.

We climbed up the side of the train.

We jumped in.

"Wow, it's amazing," I said.

It had one TV, two PS3 controllers and two fat boyz. We closed the roof and locked it. That's when we heard it.

"Darn."

Then: "Scar, it's locked."

Quinn quickly told me to move. He got out a key from his backpack and unlocked a hatch on the floor and pulled the bag on his back and pulled out his BB gun. He whispered: "Get yours out."

I did what he instructed.

"We're men in black," I joked.

The hatch opened to the ground, beneath there was nearly no space.

Now there were loads of kids on top hitting and screaming.

He pointed to his left. There was another train and loads of cover. But he said: "Garbage."

There was also a hole in the ground with loads of garbage.

"Three, two, one."

We both rolled out and ran.

I heard the BB bullets hit all around us.

But none hit. I jumped onto the ladder of a train and climbed onto the top.

Scar yelled: "They're too fast."

I saw Quinn just jump into the garbage pit.

He disappeared. He came back up and screamed: "Jump in!"

I was looking in the different direction to Quinn. I did a backflip into the pit.

Surprisingly under there you could breathe. I felt like I was going to puke.

It smelled like poop and there were loads of maggots.

Quinn was right there and said for me to go down deep, as then they can't get us there.

We were at the bottom listening to the faint sound of people screaming. There were sounds of people firing at us.

We just sat and waited.

There were sounds of people digging around. Quinn and I just sat there and talked. "Why did you come here?" he asked. "Because of my dad's job," I answered.

After a while we went close to the surface.

Quinn poked his head up. Nothing. I got my head out. Nothing. Quinn got out. Then *bang*. Hailfire.

I got out and loaded my gun.

I fired at them. We were getting fired at. I did a Superman roll over a wall forty five centimetres tall.

I hid behind it and fired.

Quinn wasn't so fast and got hit.

He fell backwards in pain. I kept hitting them. I pretended to call the cops. Then they ran.

I dived into the pit and started to dig around.

I got the rope out. I got out and found a place to throw the rope over then I looked at the pit looking for Quinn.

I saw a shoe just slip in.

I jumped where that was.

I tied the rope around his ankles. I jumped out and got the other end of the rope. I pulled it and Quinn came out.

I untied his ankles and checked him for where he got hit. He had a cut on the side of his face.

I got my first aid kit that's always in my bag and fixed him up.

After we decided to take a walk through town. After three hours we went home.

5. QUINN'S BIRTHDAY

I woke up and remembered it was Quinn's birthday.

I got ready and went round to his house. I rang the doorbell. He looked out the window. Then he came and opened the door.

"Happy birthday!"

His mum came to the door. We all drove to town. "How's the cut on your face?"

"It's okay - still hurts. I swear the next time I see Scar I'm going to kill him."

We went to the motocross shop.

He got a nice bike.

Quinn and I drove it the whole day.

"I've been saving for this since I was five."

"Don't break it."

I was riding it when I messed up and we went zooming. We were going 80 km on a normal road.

There was a sharp turn and we went flying on the curb.

"Slow down," Quinn screamed.

I was curving everywhere.

I was like a mad man.

I finally slowed down. We parked it and went to my dad's car shop. I asked dad if I could get a bike.

"You'll need some money son, better start saving."

Quinn and I left.

"This time I'll drive," Quinn spluttered.

We drove to the train.

Quinn went up to it and stuck a key in a side door. It opened up to the cockpit that had been transformed into a garage. He had spray painted the glass so you couldn't see in.

He drove his bike in.

We went in.

"I brought some stuff," I said.

I brought a little fire charge and a camera. We burnt a hole in the wall and stuck the camera near the hole. Then I plugged the camera wire in the TV.

When we did there was a little screen at the top right corner. We saw Scar coming. We quickly got on the bike.

I got my BB gun out.

"Won't they get in if we don't lock the door?" I asked.

"It locks as soon as it closes," Quinn replied.

"Three, two, one."

We opened the door and we drove really fast.

I started shooting rapid fire.

Scar came zooming after us on his motocross.

He also had a guy on the back firing.

Quinn yelled: "Hold on!"

I turned forward. I held tight. There was a one metre high wall.

"How we going to get over that?"

He pointed his hand.

I saw this bit of wood on the wall.

It was not very steep though.

Quinn started going really fast.

Before I knew it we were flying.

We landed. It hurt my bum.

Scar was still behind us.

Eventually he stopped following us.

We followed him. We ended up at a foster home.

He got off and walked in.

I got off and started walking around the side. I looked through the window.

There was a little girl. "Hi sis," said Scar.

I ran back to Quinn. I hopped on his bike. "Go!"

We went and I told Quinn what I had heard. "He has a sister and he lives in a foster home? Since when?"

"Let's go home," Quinn said with astonishment.

We went home.

6. THE DEN

"Hey Quinn."

"What's up?"

"Let's go to the den."

"Have you got the stuff?"

"Yeah Quinn."

We went to the train. We got our spray paints. We spray painted the train. Then we went in the train.

We got the very cheap cameras out.

We cut and burnt holes in the walls.

Then we set up a computer.

We could look at the computer to check out if anyone was coming.

We made small holes that we could stick the end of our BB guns through.

I brought some PlayStation games.

We played for hours.

"Again here comes Scar," said Quinn.

"Yeah, let's show him who's boss," I replied. "I forgot to tell you. I brought a few cherry bombs to get him back for what he did to you."

I got my sling shot, cherry bombs and my BB gun out.

I put three cherry bombs and fired them. *Bang, bang, bang.*

I fired more and more and more.

Then I pulled my BB gun out.

Quinn and I rapid fired them.

They started to retreat.

"Let's run for it. They'll come back soon."

We got out, locked everything and ran for it. We ran and ran. We got to town.

Then I realised they were there behind us.

"Run!"

Quinn and I ran for the stairs, we raced up the stairs.

"How fast are they?" Scar screamed. "Especially the new kid."

We kept running till we reached the roof. Then we just stood there. Scar came.

"Look who we have here. Now you're mine…," said Scar. "Get them!"

The gang ran at us.

Quinn and I turned. We ran. There was a big drop then a building. I ran and jumped.

I was falling. Then I felt it, the sharp pain in my legs.

It was really painful. I saw Quinn jump and land next to me. We landed on a balcony.

We jumped to the one below, then the other.

We were about ten metres from the ground. There was the river.

I jumped. I felt the water come all around me.

I swam to the shore. I got out with Quinn.

"We got away," I croaked.

"You're crazy - you'll get us killed one day," said Quinn.

We ran back to our houses to get dry.

Quinn and I met on the road 20 minutes later.

"Hey look it's a cat," I said.

We ran to the cat. We were stroking him. Scar came and screamed: "There's a cat!"

He ran away.

"He's scared of cats!" I howled with laughter.

I thought that was crazy - a kid like him scared of cats.

Now, if he's scared of cats what else is he scared of I asked myself.

We went after him. "Where did he go?" Quinn asked.

"To the right," I answered.

We were running at full pace. I was faster than Quinn.

Scar was sprinting. We were catching up. I turned on my turbo boost and ran right at him.

I got close and rugby tackled him.

He was on the ground. Quinn was there in a matter of seconds.

"So Scar, you're scared of cats," I said.

Quinn raced off and came back with a cat in his hands.

"Tell me how you know where we are. 'Cause you're always coming by when we're in those places."

"I've got my ways," he whimpered.

"Tell me, or my friend Quinn here will drop the cat right on you."

"Fine, I've got hidden cameras. Now let me go."

I got his bag and rustled through it.

There was this mini screen in his bag. I turned it on, there were the cameras. I saw a button saying 'delete'. I pressed it and all the tiny movies were gone.

"Let's go Quinn," I said.

7. THE TEAM

It was one day before school started.

I woke up on a Monday morning. I got my running things on.

I was joining a running team.

When I got there I saw Quinn running round the track.

I went down and a man came up to me.

"Who's this young man?"

"I'm Scott."

I went down to the track.

"Okay I need to know how fast you are and put you in a group. You'll be doing one hundred metres. Three, two, one, go!"

I started running.

Before I knew it I was at the hundred metre line.

I was out of breath.

"You're real fast. You beat the club record. You got 13.68 seconds."

I started training. Everyone was coming for high fives and autographs.

"I wasn't that fast. My best is 12.99."

When training was finished I ran to Quinn.

"Dude, how did you go that fast?" he said in astonishment.

"I practised," I replied.

We ran home together.

When we got home I asked Quinn over. We both went to my place.

We went to my bedroom and opened the window.

I climbed out onto the roof. Quinn followed me up. I had built a base up there. I opened the hatch and in we went.

I had one of my big BB guns there. It had a scope on it.

"When Scar comes to our houses we can climb up here and fire," I laughed and down the road he came. What a coincidence, I thought.

I got the BB gun and looked through the scope.

I aimed right at his butt. I fired. "I wonder when he'll just leave us alone," I said.

Scar was now on the floor wailing. I took aim and fired at him again and again and again.

They still didn't see my hiding spot. I aimed at his fellow gang mates and fired at them. I started singing "....and another one bites the dust. And another one down, another one down, another one bites the dust".

Then Quinn started screaming. "Ah, are you ready? Another one bites the dust!"

Now they spotted us because of his screaming.

They were all firing at us. I closed the firing hatch.

I opened the back hole out. I crawled out. I went over the ridge on the roof. I was going down the other side. I heard the kids running to the other side to get us.

We had a trampoline in the garden. I jumped off our roof onto the trampoline.

Because our house was a double decker house it was a high drop.

When I landed, I bounced off it and flew over the hedge. I landed on the other side.

My ankle ached but it wasn't bad.

Quinn landed. We started running. I got to the road and legged it.

They were on our tails already. I ran into the forest.

Quinn screamed at me to stop. He screamed "there's a drop", but I kept running.

There it was - the drop he was screaming about. I didn't have time to stop. I jumped.

It felt like slow motion in mid-air. I landed on the other side. I thought I was there but I was 20 metres from the top. Scar landed right there in front. He slipped. I quickly grabbed him before he dropped. I pulled him up.

"You okay?" I asked.

"Yeah. Why did you help me, midget?" he replied.

I started to climb out. I got to the top. I ran away.

Quinn was there waiting.

All of a sudden Scar's gang jumped out at me.

Quinn and I were caught. "Where's Scar?" called a kid called Hunter. He was Scar's henchman.

"Well, I offered him help but he just flicked me away. He's in the ravine. Can we leave now?" I asked.

"Not until Scar comes," Hunter replied. But he nodded his head. I wondered what it meant. I turned around and four of his guys were leaping at us.

I was quick to side step. They were faster. They were on me in seconds. I punched one and he rolled free but the other one was still on me. Quinn was up already and the kids that jumped on him were on the floor. Quinn got the kid off me in three touches. I stood up.

I looked around. They were all there ready to jump on us. I quickly drew my BB gun.

I shot at three of the guys next to each other. They jumped to the side. I ran through the gap.

Quinn was on other people. He beat two up and ran. "Where did you learn to fight?" I asked.

"Karate. I used to go to karate class."

I looked at him in astonishment. We kept running. I stopped and looked behind.

Scar's gang were all running to the forest. Two of them were on their bikes chasing us though.

I told Quinn. I sprinted off into a side lane. Quinn kept going down the same street. One of the bike guys chased me.

Up ahead I saw scaffolding in one hundred metres. I was sprinting with all the energy I had. The bike was so close.

He was about to catch me. I could not get away.

There was the scaffolding. I jumped up and started to climb up the side of the scaffolding.

The kid got off his bike and started climbing after me.

At the top there was a wet sponge to clean the roof. I picked it up and dropped it on the kid.

The kid fell off.

Luckily he was just one metre from the ground. He looked like he was fine. "Next time you'll think twice about chasing me, you loser," I screamed down to him.

I ran. I saw three kids on Quinn. He was down and they each had BB guns. I got my BB gun out and shot at them.

One of them ran and dived behind a wall.

The other ran the other way and jumped into one of the wrecked buildings. I hit the other one twice and he rolled on the floor.

The other ones were shooting at me. Quinn got away and legged it to the scaffolding. He got up and then was with me.

Two more kids arrived and they came to the scaffolding.

"Quinn - we've got two options. One, we stay here and keep firing until they run or they get us. Two, we run and we'll jump over the drops between buildings."

"Number two I'd say," Quinn said.

We ran and jumped over the drops. We kept running - we could not be stopped. The kids that were climbing had now reached the top of the ten metre building.

They ducked and fired at us. One got lucky and hit me. I fell flat on my face. Quinn stopped and pulled out his gun. He fired at them. We were two buildings apart. I pulled myself together and fired as well.

"Argh, it hurts," I shrieked. I was really pumped up now.

The other guys were climbing up where the others were. I whispered: "I'll say I'm out of bullets and you say same. Then those guys will come and I'll break their bones.!

"I'm out of bullets!" I screamed. "Me too!" Quinn screamed.

The kids started running at us. I stood up and they kept coming. The first one came and stood there.

The other one came. I ran at them and before they could blink I shot them both from close range and ran.

"Let's go too far for their range," I said.

We kept running. The buildings kept getting smaller.

We were just three metres from the ground now. The next jump was big. I stopped and waited.

"Let's jump off now, there's a big bin container," I said.

I jumped in and Quinn came in too.

I closed the lid.

I turned on my flashlight. We sat in anticipation.

We heard their footsteps closer.

"Do you think they know we're here?" Quinn asked.

"No, don't think so," I replied.

There were no more footsteps, then the satisfying thud of them landing on the other building and keeping running.

I got out and walked away.

Quinn followed.

We went down to the right. That was the way to town. When we got there we were greeted by a big market.

They were selling everything. We were walking through. I saw a food stand. We went over and bought two slices of pizza.

"Hey, why do you think Scar keeps chasing us?" I asked Quinn.

"Well I think he's jealous of you," he answered.

We were walking through when we heard someone scream.

I ran to the scream. There was a man robbing an old lady. He ran away. I was right after him in a few seconds.

"Quinn call the police," I screamed over my shoulder.

Quinn was chasing me with his phone.

He was talking to the police. I was catching the man. I tackled him.

He was on the floor and fighting. I was struggling to keep him under control. He was a strong man.

But I remembered, it wasn't the boy in the fight, it was the fight in the boy. The police had come. They took him away.

8. THE HERO

The police brought me home in a car.

They were all questioning Quinn and me. I told them everything.

We pulled up at Quinn and my house. His parents and mine were in the kitchen with the officers.

Quinn and I were playing in my room.

We saw Scar come down the road and he saw the peacekeeper's car and ran.

Then they called us down.

"Today you two have done something very good," said one of the officers. "You two are only young. You could get yourself very hurt. Please be careful next time. But we would like to thank you. You saved one thousand dollars' worth of things in that granny's bag. The very kind lady at the mall gave us two hundred dollars. You each get one hundred for doing that."

"Thanks, bye officer," I replied. I went back up and saw Scar just at the wall of our neighbour's house. He was by himself.

"What have you done wrong now kid?" he screamed at me.

"Look what the officers gave me." I waved the money.

I closed the window and put the money in my piggy bank.

I was happy with my winnings but now Scar would want it off me.

My piggy bank had a code so Scar wouldn't get in but he would keep trying.

I hid my piggy bank under my bed. I turned on my radio and sat back on my bed. I was on my iPod thinking about tomorrow.

It was the first day of school. It was only one in the afternoon.

I decided to go to town and see what I could get. I was looking around because Scar could be following. I was just minding my own business when three men came up to me.

"Why'd you scumbag tackle my friend? Now he's in court and could well go to prison. I would just like you to come with me so I can teach you a lesson," said one of the men.

The other two that weren't talking came behind me and pushed me forward. I was kind of worried about what would happen.

They took me down under the ground into a basement.

I thought to myself, I haven't even gone to school yet and two gangs already hate me.

Great.

They tied me to a chair. He got a big light and shone it on my face. I was sitting there. He screamed: "Don't mess things up for people. It's none of your business."

Then he let me go. I was wondering why he went through all the hassle just to tell me that. I walked around. I saw all these cool things. I saw the sign for school.

I ran to it.

It was a big building next to the river. I was excited to go to school but nervous.

I went up to the gates. I went through the gates. I went up to the door. I looked in.

There was a teacher coming. I ran. I ran out of the gates and kept running. I didn't want to have a bad start. I ran back to the market then I kept running. I ran all the way to my dad's garage. I went in.

"Hey dad. What class am I in again?" I asked.

I just saw the teacher's name tag. It was a lady. It said 'Mrs Gol...' I didn't get to see the rest. My dad said "Mrs Golding". Man, that lady at the front was probably Mrs Golding, I thought to myself.

9. SCHOOL

It was seven thirty in the morning.
First day of school.

I got up and got dressed. I got my
school bag. It had everything I
needed. I went downstairs. My sister
was there.

I hadn't seen her for the whole
holiday.

She was 18. Five years older than I
was.

She had been at college while I was on holiday. Now it was her holiday. I had breakfast.

"Good luck honey. Have a good first day," my mum called when I was walking out the door.

It was now seven fifty. School started at eight. I got on my bike.

Quinn came out.

"What class are you in Quinn?"

"Mrs Golding's."

"Nice, me too."

We left off together. I was biking at full speed with Quinn.

"Good thing Scar's in upper school."

"Yeah," Quinn replied.

We pulled up at the school gates.

I locked up my bike at the front door with my padlock.

I walked in. There were people everywhere.

There were two minutes before class. We went to our lockers.

I put some of my stuff in.

"How come we're always next to each other?" I asked Quinn.

"Because we're the coolest. Just kidding. What's your last name?" he said.

"Bolt. What's yours?"

"Black," Quinn said.

"That's why. Let's start walking to class."

We got to class thirty seconds before school started.

We walked in. School started. "So class, let's start by introducing ourselves," said Mrs Golding.

Kids started to say what their name was, where they came from and if there was something special about them. It was my turn. "My name is Scott. I'm from England."

Now it was Quinn.

"My name is Quinn. I'm also from England."

Then we went to our desks.

There were 18 kids in our class. There were three at a table. These were going to be the tables for the year.

"Everyone get into groups of threes," said Mrs Golding.

There were these two kids asking me to be in their group, but I wanted to be with Quinn. So I walked up to Quinn. We kept asking kids but they seemed to already have friends.

Eventually there was only one girl left. She was also new. We had to join her.

She was a new girl from the US. Her name was Lexi. She seemed nice.

We had to do this group building stuff.

After it was art.

We had to draw a portrait of the people in our group but just one.

I had to do Lexi, Quinn did me and Lexi did Quinn. She had blonde hair and blue eyes.

I drew a fairly good drawing of her.

We had to work on this next week.

After it was already lunch.

It was burgers and French fries.

In the queue I asked Lexi: "What are French fries?" She looked at me like I was an idiot.

"Oh yeah, you're English, umm they're..umm, what do you call them? Oh, chips."

"Thanks."

Then we went to recess.

Quinn and I went to play football and Lexi followed.

She screamed: "See you after lunch Scott!"

We played football. I got the ball and out dribbled all of them, I shot and scored. Their team scored.

Quinn was nearly as good as I was. We got kicked off the field for the last ten minutes of recess.

These kids kept coming up to Quinn and I, and kept saying how good we were.

Next it was PE. I was excited. I was good at my old school.

When we arrived there were people playing dodgeball. I really loved dodgeball. I ran in. I picked up a ball and chucked it right at someone.

I looked at the person I hit. His face was red with rage. He was out but I could tell when he came back in he would batter me.

I was the last one in my team but I was confident I was going to catch a ball. I saw my opportunity. There was a ball coming slowly right at me. It swerved to my right. I dived. I caught it, then dropped it. I was out. Now everyone was upset with me.

The guy that threw the ball turned out to be the main bully.

So he didn't like me. Now no-one liked me. Great.

Quinn came up to me. "Fail. Now everyone hates you, lol."

"Quinn, stop rubbing it in my face."

I walked off with red cheeks and my head in my hands. I went to the bathroom. I washed my face. After school I went to the running track. I ran for one hour. My phone started to ring. I picked it up. It was Quinn.

"Hey Scott, where have you been? I've looked everywhere for you," he said.

"Dude, you were a jerk. Friends aren't jerks to each other," I said.

"Sorry, dude I messed up but I didn't mean to upset you."

I hung up. He called again but I hung up straight away. I started to run up the road. I was heading home. I got in and ran straight to my room.

10. THE WEEKEND

"That week of school wasn't the best. I mean, I got in trouble thirteen times. I got in three fights and I got a black eye," I said while sitting on the back of Quinn's bike.

We were going to the paintball warfare ground.

When we got there, there was also another group. I went up to the paintball guy.

"When can I play with my friend here?" I asked.

"Now if you want to go up against those guys."

"Scott, no," said Quinn.

"Yeah they're on." I got on all my stuff.

Quinn and me against 15 kids.

I only just realised it was Scar's gang we were against when I entered the forest/warfare ground. I got ready.

Beep.

The game began. If you got hit you were out.

I ran behind a tree and moved forward.

I could hear but didn't see them coming. I looked round my tree.

I saw them now. About one hundred metres off.

I aimed and fired.

Bang.

I didn't get them.

I messed up my cover. I looked out and fired more and more.

They were very close.

I finally hit one.

He was out. I realised I hadn't seen Quinn.

I hit another and another.

Right now I was relying on luck. I got on my tummy and moved forward.

I was behind a pile of fallen down trees.

I poked my head up. I saw more men there. I had taken three but there were eight more.

I aimed and fired. I put it on rapid fire.

I was now just firing at them without control.

I hit three more.

Where was Quinn?

I had got six out of 15.

I fired more and more.

I had no more targets left because I just hit two.

Then I saw Quinn.

"I hit eight," I cried out. "I hit six," said Quinn.

Scar was the last, I could tell.

Now we were the two prey and he was the predator. I looked around.

Bang, bang, bang, bang, bang, bang. Quinn had been hit.

I saw him now.

He looked like he didn't know where I was.

I aimed and fired. I was flying in slow motion to me.

"No!"

I had hit Scar. We won. We left the arena.

When I got out Lexi was there.

I wondered why.

"Robert," she called.

Scar came up to her. I wondered why.

11. THE TRUTH

When I arrived at school I ran straight to class and sat down where Lexi was. "Lexi, do you know Scar and why did you call him Robert?" I asked.

"He's my brother. His real name is Robert and why do you care?" she said.

"Well, umm. He and I are like enemies. Thinking about it, you do look like the girl at the foster home."

"Yeah, we live there. I'm only new because I went to a different school. I can't say much more without telling stuff *Robert* doesn't let me."

For the rest of the day I was baffled. I wondered why a kid like Scar had secrets to hide.

I met Quinn at lunch. I told him everything. After school Quinn and I followed Lexi. We followed her to the foster home.

Then we went to the window and we saw them. I saw them both.

"Don't tell those two brats anything!" he screamed.

He pushed Lexi over.

She started to cry. "If it wasn't for you I wouldn't have this scar!" he screamed.

I wondered what he meant. I kept listening. Then they left. I pushed the window.

Luckily it was open. I was scared. Quinn and I started walking to the door when it flew open.

There was a kid. No older than three. I luckily had some sweeties and threw them outside and locked the door behind him when he got out.

"Never know, he might get back in," I said.

We moved out. We heard screaming from upstairs. We walked up the stairs. When we got to the top I listened. "It's that door there," I said.

We walked up.

"If it gets out that I tripped over a little girl at one of the foster chances and got the scar I'll be a laughing stock." I heard from inside the room.

There was a kid walking up the stairs.

He looked ten. He screamed when he saw us.

The door flung open. Scar was there.

"You!" he screamed.

He pushed me back. I fell but stood up and ran.

Quinn chased after me. We were at the front door when two of Scar's men got on us. I punched one and kicked the other.

We ran out the door.

Now Scar was close.

Scar's crew was right out front. I was shocked. I didn't have enough time to slow down.

I side stepped the first two but the other one tackled me. I was down on the floor.

People were on me. Quinn was more successful. He was through.

"Run. Keep running for ever!" I screamed. "Don't stop until you get home. Don't come get me. Stay away from this!"

That was the last time I saw Quinn. He was gone. I got carried and dumped in the basement. I was stuck there.

Two guys were at the door. My hands and feet were tied.

Scar came down with Lexi. Lexi was crying.

"You better answer me or I'll hurt my sis Lexi here. First question - where will Quinn go?"

"I don't know. He just left."

I really didn't know. He shoved Lexi down.

"I'll find your friend. I will," he screamed as he left.

The two guards went out and closed and locked the door.

They were on the outside. I nodded my head at my feet.

"Untie them," I whispered.

"Go to my bag and get my clippers and cut this wire so I can get out."

She was back and snipped my hands and feet free. I got up, got my bag and got my BB gun out. I also got my rope out. There was a window.

I went up to it. I opened it. It was about three metres from the ground.

I threw the rope up. It went over the slit on the drain. I had two ends of the rope.

I tied one of the ends to my waist. I pulled on the other end. I was moving up with my BB gun in my mouth.

I got to the top. Then I got Lexi to climb in the window and pull the rope. Now I was hovering.

I got my BB gun and shot the guys at the front door. "Get me down!" I said. Lexi let me down slowly. We quickly got back in.

The guys on guard opened the door to check if we were still there. I fired. I hit them both and they fell.

They were both shocked and didn't make a sound.

I took their BB guns.

I had two. I gave one to Lexi. I ran up the stairs. Lexi followed. I ran.

"Lexi go hide somewhere. It's not safe with me," I said.

I ran right to the train. Quinn was there and pulled me in. We locked everything. "It was like hell in there man. I swear. I was scared sick. Anyway, Scar and his gang are after us. If he finds us we're in big trouble." We then left. We ran and ran. We eventually got to our houses.

12. THE TRUTH

We were the champions of the school.

The next morning we left. We were heading for the foster home. We were taking a risk of tracking Scar down. We were not scared of Scar anymore.

We were going to take the fight to him.

We saw him. He was running out of the foster home and he had eight men behind him.

"Where are you two morons?" he screamed.

I pulled my BB gun. I ran across the drive behind the hedge on the other side. I shot at them.

Bang, bang, bang.

They fired back.

Now there were BB bullets firing everywhere.

Bang, bang, bang, bang, bang, bang.

Now we were in for a fight.

We were going to take him down.

His men were getting into hiding spots to fire. I knew this was my chance. I ran and jumped on Scar, he was down in a flash. I took a photo.

It felt like I was covered in bruises.

I gave the all clear sign to Quinn and we legged it.

We ran all the way home. I ran into my house, up the stairs and into my bedroom.

Quinn and I sat down looked at the photo.

"Perfect," I said.

We printed it hundreds of times with the words 'did little sis trip you up and give you another scar?' at the bottom.

It was school the next day. The picture was the perfect way to knock Scar down. Everyone was laughing and knew the truth.

"Hey Lexi," I said.

She just walked right past me.

It felt like a bullet had just hit me.

All the kids were cheering. They loved how we had made Scar look like a loser.

13. AFTER

Two weeks later.

Scar was not a bully anymore.

Quinn and I were the most popular kids in the school.

Lexi started to talk to me again.

I ran my first tournament for Detroit. I came first.

We won one thousand dollars.

That paid for us to have a better running track. Quinn came second, winning five hundred dollars.

I got a motocross bike. All the gangs that had bullied us were now nice.

In England Jack now had a new friend called Quinn as well.

And I will live to tell the tale.

Craig Ditchfield has lived in Switzerland since he was born and is ten-years-old. He is originally from England and Scotland. He has lived in three houses in Switzerland. He loves to read and his favourite authors are Robert Muchamore, author of the best-selling 'Cherub' series, and Michael Grant, author of the best-selling 'Gone' series. He loves to play rugby, basketball and wouldn't miss a chance to ski. He has a lovely 13-year-old sister who is amazing at swimming and called Katie, the two best parents in the world and a big flat coated retriever called Archie.

Made in the USA
Las Vegas, NV
18 January 2023

65817635R00049